Granny's Baseball Book

By Agnes N. Hopps

AuthorHouse™
1663 Liberty Drive
Bloomington, IN 47403
www.authorhouse.com
Phone: 1-800-839-8640

First published by AuthorHouse 11/16/2011

ISBN: 978-1-4634-0676-9 (sc)

Library of Congress Control Number: 2011917102

Printed in the United States of America

Any people depicted in stock imagery provided by Thinkstock are models,
and such images are being used for illustrative purposes only.
Certain stock imagery © Thinkstock.

This book is printed on acid-free paper.

authorHOUSE®

Once there was a little boy named Jordan. Jordan was a smart and happy little boy. He loved his mommy and his granny, whom he lived with. One day he was sitting on his front steps

"I guess you can," said Davon. "My dad is going to teach me to play baseball. He said, "He did not want me to be just a batboy on the team. The batboy does not get to hit the ball or play. All he does is hand the player their bats. And I want to play. So I am going to learn to play so I can be picked."

"I can learn to play too," said Jordan. "Will your Dad teach me too," he asked?

Jordan thought about it, I could learn to be a baseball player too. But who will teach me. I cannot wait for Davon's father to teach me. I may not get to play.

Jordan went into the house to his mom. "Mommy, I want to learn how to play baseball," he said.

"Hey, that's good, I was a pitcher when I was in high school," she said.

"But Davon's father is going to teach him so he will not be a batboy who does not get to play. Can Mommy teach baseball for a boy's teams?"

Jordan smiled and went to his grandmother's room sat down in her big rocking chair and began to think.

Granny looked up from what she was doing. "You're thinking pretty hard over there. What's wrong?" She said.

"Davon's father is going to teach Davon to play baseball.

"But Granny, I want to read the baseball book now. Can you write me one, please," he said.

"I have written many books but a baseball book. I do not know if I can write a baseball book." she said.

"First we need to learn the shapes of baseball," she said.

"Why shape, Granny? Why do we need to learn shapes?"

She said, "Well if you know the shapes of baseball you will

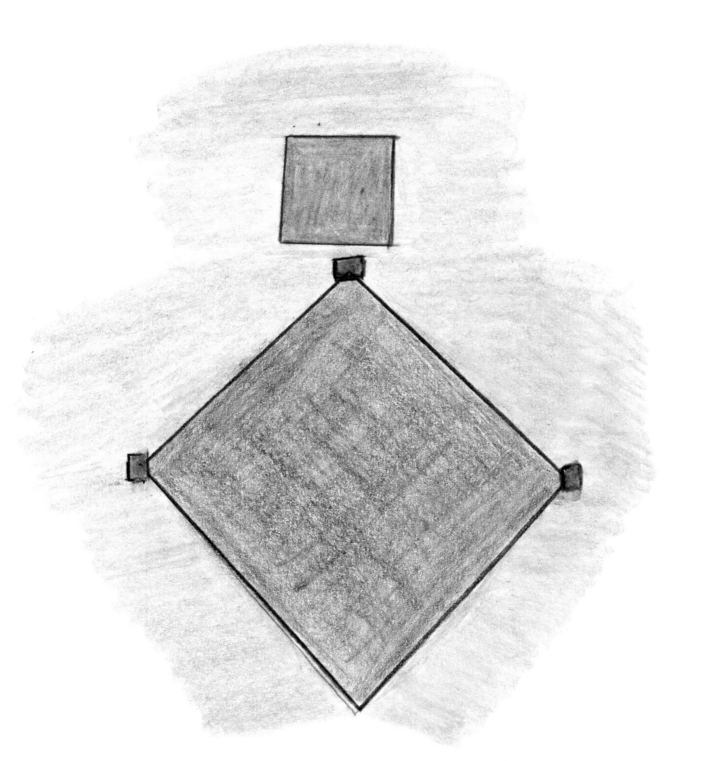

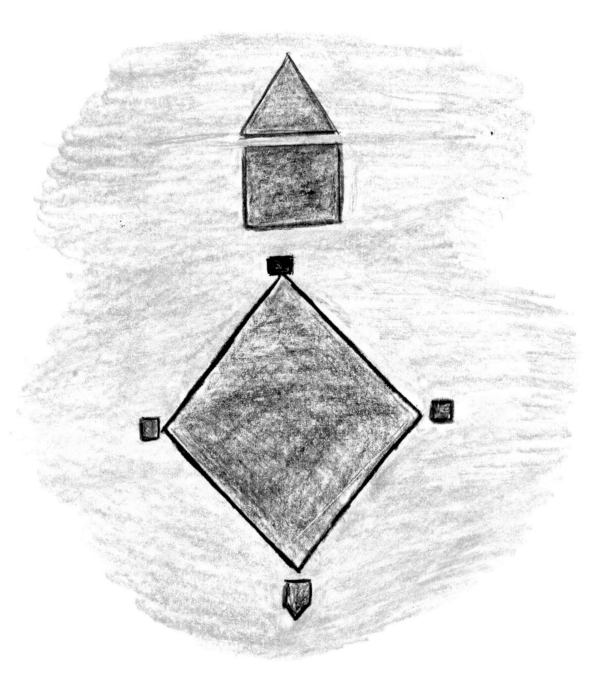

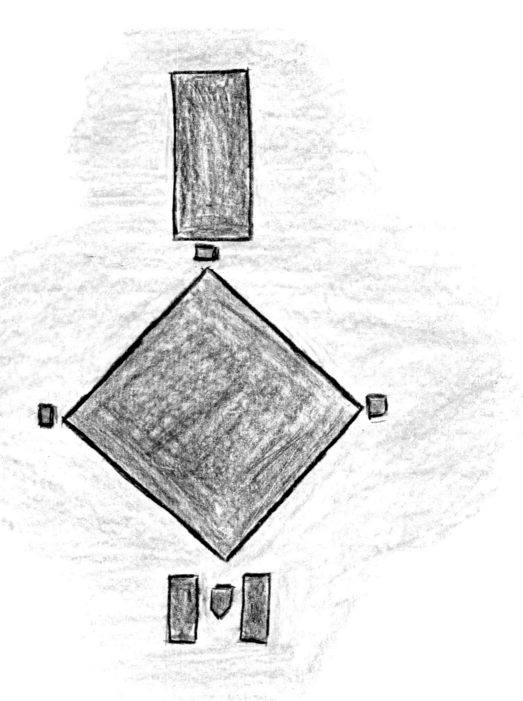

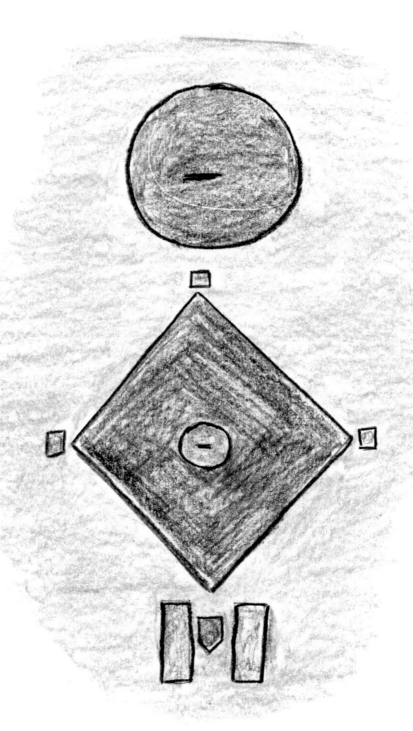

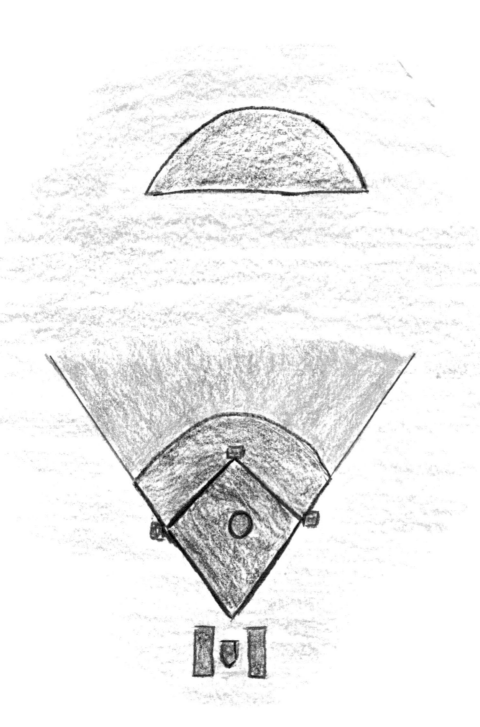

"Now there is one more shape you need to know and

"Now you know all the shapes of the game. Let see who the players are. First there is the batter. He stands in the batter's box. If he is right-handed he stands in the left box. If

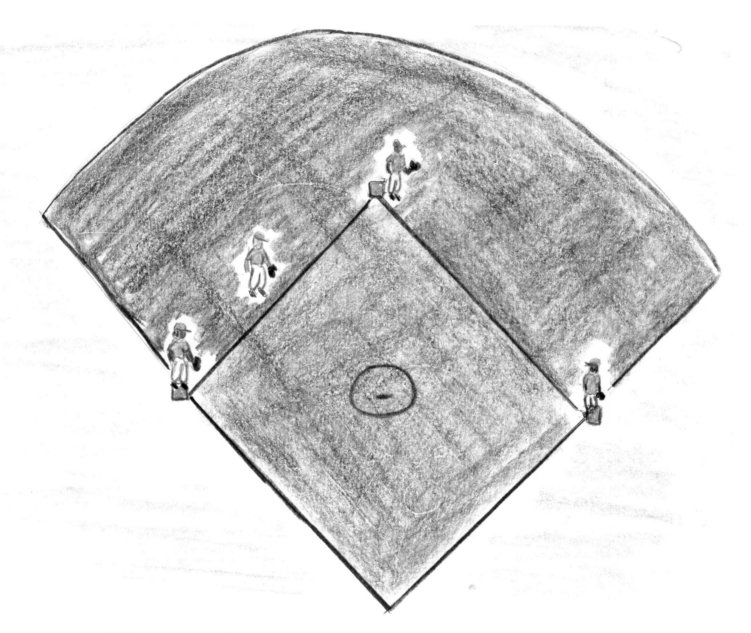

"There are the infielders. There is a man on each of the bases. There's the first baseman for the first base, the second baseman for the second base and the third baseman for the third base. The first and third basemen stand on their base to catch any balls that are hit his way. The second baseman

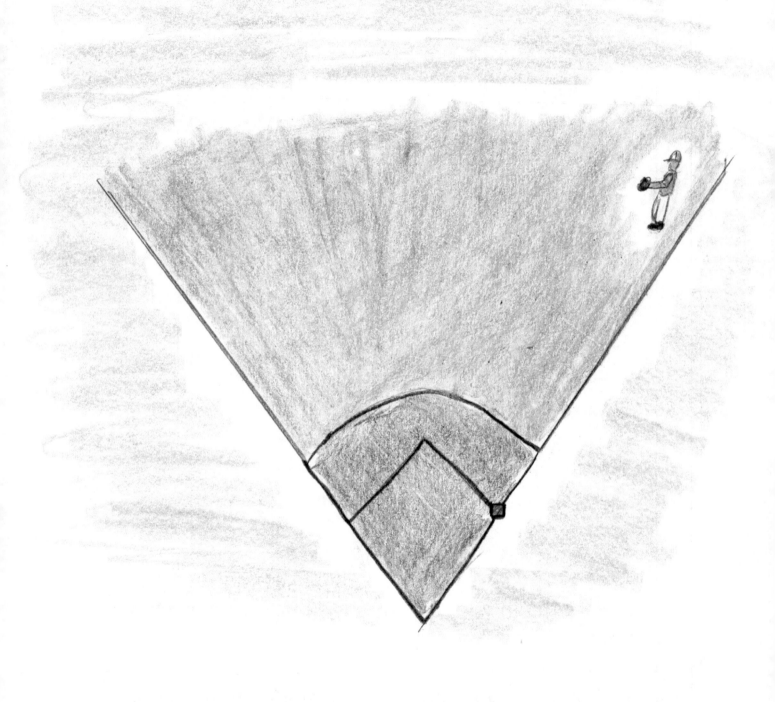

"And…" said Granny, turning around from her desk to find Jordan asleep in the chair. "Well, I guess my baseball book was so exciting that you went to sleep. I won't be making any money on this." She laughed and put the few sheets of paper of the baseball book on her desk. She then took the sleepy Jordan to bed.

The next day Jordan went to his mommy. "Mommy, can you teach me how to hit? I know all about baseball now. Granny wrote a baseball book for me," he said holding up the pages of the little book.

"She did!" Mommy said looking a little surprised. "I did not know Granny knew much about baseball."

"And practice is just what they did. Every day for two weeks Jordan wanted to hit and hit and hit. Sometime Mommy had to turn on the back yard lights because Jordan did not want to stop. One night it was getting late and Jordan did not want to stop practice.

"We can practice tomorrow Jordan, it is late and dark. We have to go inside now," she said.

Mommy looked at Jordan for a little bit, and then she pitched him a ball right down to home plate. Jordan swung as hard as he could. He hit the ball it flew high in the sky and up over the house.

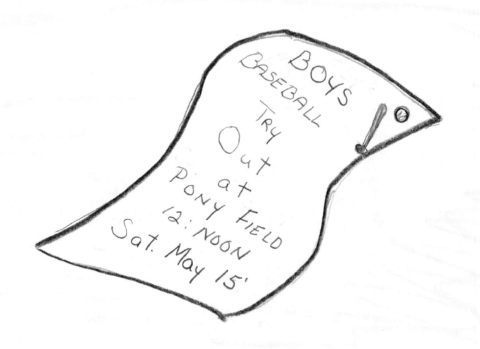

"Well, let's see," pulling a paper out of her pants pocket. "It says here the try outs will be Saturday two weeks away. I think you are ready, do you think you can wait until then," she asked?

"Saturday two weeks is a long time away. But I got things to do until then," he said. "Are we going to be practicing some more," she asked?

"No, I got to read Granny's Baseball book over and over

"Ok, but can you catch a ball? A good player has to know how to catch and hit," she smiled.

"Catch! We did not practice catching can you teach me to catch, too," he asked.

The next two weeks Mommy and Granny threw balls for
Jordan to catch. Mommy would hit balls high up in the air for
him to catch. This was the hardest of all to learn. For the ball
look like it would hit him. He would duck to keep the ball from

The day came for the tryouts. Jordan, his Mommy and his Granny got in the car and drove to the field. There were a lot of cars. There were a lot of dads and sons standing around a tall man with a clip-broad in his hand.

"Come on Jordan let's sign you up for the try outs," his mother said.

"Mom, do you think I will be picked. All those boys had their dads to help them to learn baseball. What if I do not make the team," he said.

"If you do your best and they do not pick you, then it is

Jordan and his Mom walked over to the tall man with the clipboard. Jordan's mom put Jordan's name on the list. Jordan's mom kissed the top of his head and whispered, "Remember you have something no other boy has, you have a Granny's Baseball Book."

"Now," the man said, "let's see what you guys know about baseball."

Jordan raised his hand for the first question. He raised his hand for the second question. He looked back at his Mom and smiled. He had his Granny's Baseball Book, with all the